The Chicken Egg-splosion

Pigs CAN fly!

Kweeeeeeeeeeeeeeeeeeeeeeeeep!

When the Alarm Squeal sounds it must
be a job for Captain Peter Porker and
the PIGS IN PLANES!

Paul Cooper is from Manchester.
He now lives in Cambridge with
his wife and two daughters.

*Read these high-flying adventures
about the Pigs in Planes:*

PIGS IN PLANES: THE CHICKEN EGG-SPLOSION
PIGS IN PLANES: THE SHARK BITES BACK

The Chicken Egg-splosion

PAUL COOPER

Illustrated by Trevor Dunton

PUFFIN

PUFFIN BOOKS

Published by the Penguin Group
Penguin Books Ltd, 80 Strand, London WC2R 0RL, England
Penguin Group (USA) Inc., 375 Hudson Street, New York, New York 10014, USA
Penguin Group (Canada), 90 Eglinton Avenue East, Suite 700, Toronto, Ontario, Canada M4P 2Y3
(a division of Pearson Penguin Canada Inc.)
Penguin Ireland, 25 St Stephen's Green, Dublin 2, Ireland (a division of Penguin Books Ltd)
Penguin Group (Australia), 250 Camberwell Road, Camberwell, Victoria 3124, Australia
(a division of Pearson Australia Group Pty Ltd)
Penguin Books India Pvt Ltd, 11 Community Centre, Panchsheel Park, New Delhi – 110 017, India
Penguin Group (NZ), 67 Apollo Drive, Rosedale, North Shore 0632, New Zealand
(a division of Pearson New Zealand Ltd)
Penguin Books (South Africa) (Pty) Ltd, 24 Sturdee Avenue, Rosebank, Johannesburg 2196, South Africa

Penguin Books Ltd, Registered Offices: 80 Strand, London WC2R 0RL, England

puffinbooks.com

First published 2010
1

Text copyright © Paul Cooper, 2010
Illustrations copyright © Trevor Dunton, 2010
All rights reserved

The moral right of the author and illustrator has been asserted

Set in Bembo Infant
Made and printed in England by Clays Ltd, St Ives plc

British Library Cataloguing in Publication Data
A CIP catalogue record for this book is available from the British Library

ISBN: 978-0-141-32840-9

www.greenpenguin.co.uk

Penguin Books is committed to a sustainable future
for our business, our readers and our planet.
The book in your hands is made from paper
certified by the Forest Stewardship Council.

To Shannon and Finlay, with thanks

MEET THE CREW

PEREGRINE OINKS-GRUNTINGTON,

Wing Commander

LOLA PENN,

Radio Operator

PETER PORKER,

Captain

TAMMY SNUFFLES,

Mechanic

BRIAN TROTTER,

Medical Officer

CURLY McHOGLET,

Trainee

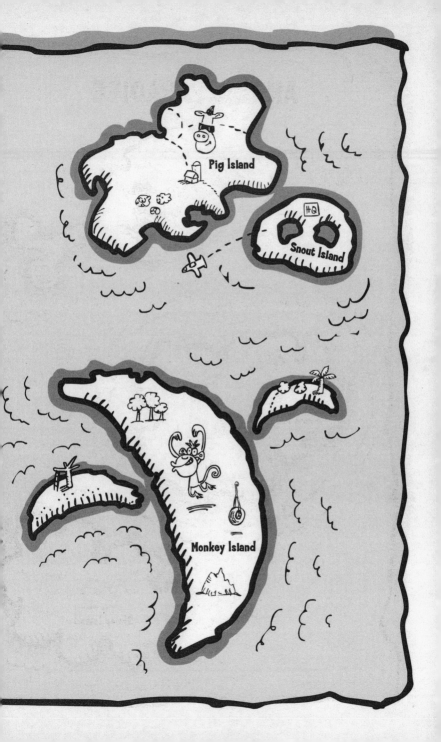

CHAPTER 1:

PiPs are GO!

'So you want to join the Pigs in Planes, do you?' boomed Wing Commander Peregrine Oinks-Gruntington. He stared down at Curly McHoglet and fed himself another chocolate biscuit through his gigantic white moustache.

Curly took a deep breath. 'More than anything in the world.'

Peregrine pointed a trotter at a stack of letters on his desk. 'And that's why you have written to us ninety-seven times asking to join?'

Curly nodded eagerly. 'I've wanted to join

the PiPs ever since I was little. The PiPs motto was the first thing I ever said – *Pigs CAN fly*. I started flying lessons as soon as I could.'

'There's more to being a PiP than just flying,' said Peregrine. 'Our lads have to be ready for anything.'

'AND our girls,' muttered the Wing Commander's assistant, Lola Penn, as she put some papers on his desk. As usual, Lola wasn't wearing a PiPs uniform. She had on a T-shirt with the words FUTURE PIGGY SUPERSTAR in sparkly letters. She rolled her eyes and left the room.

The Wing Commander went to the open window and stood there, his moustache rustling gently in the breeze. 'Come and look here, lad.'

PiPs HQ sat right between the two lakes in the middle of Snout Island. Curly had never actually been to this small island off the coast of Pig Island before, but he knew the place well because he had read everything about it.

Next to the air control tower, the famous PiPs SkyHog jets stood on the runway. A mechanic was working on one of the planes' engines, a different tool sticking out of every pocket of her oil-stained overalls.

'If there's an emergency on Emu Island or a catastrophe on Cat Island, those jets can be there in minutes,' said the Wing Commander. 'The PiPs have to be ready at any time. See that pig working on the lead jet? That's Tammy Snuffles. She's the best mechanic in the business.'

The Wing Commander demolished another choccy bicky and pointed to a second building beyond the runway. A pig sat at one window with glasses halfway down his snout and a thick book in his trotters.

'See him? That's Brian Trotter, our medical officer,' said the Wing Commander. 'It's not by chance that the letters of his first name can be rearranged to spell the word BRAIN. He's probably studying the different kinds of fungus on all the islands of Animal Paradise, or something brainy like that.' The Wing Commander looked down at the young pig. 'You see, at any moment, the PiPs must be ready for anything. That's the rule – and I'm a stickler for rules.'

'What about Captain Peter Porker?' asked Curly.

The Wing Commander's moustache

twitched crossly, sending a shower of chocolate crumbs flying. 'What about him?'

'He's my hero,' Curly said, eyes shining. 'I've read about all his missions.'

'Yes, well, I'm sure Captain Porker is keeping himself fit for duty somehow,' said the Wing Commander.

But Curly wasn't listening. He was looking down at the nearer of the island's two lakes. In fact, Left Nostril Lake lay directly below the Wing Commander's first-floor office. There was a diving-board at the water's edge, and a pig was climbing up the ladder. Curly knew that handsome piggy face from loads of newspaper stories. It was Peter Porker!

The captain stood on the diving-board and hitched up his trunks. Then he charged forward and took a flying leap off the end of the board. In mid-air he tucked himself into one huge pink ball of pig and yelled,

'CANNONBALL!'

SPLOOSH! Water exploded everywhere. Curly hopped back just in time, but the Wing Commander wasn't so fast. A pig-sized wave of lake water hit him in the snout. Water dripped from his uniform and his glorious moustache now drooped tragically.

'Captain Porker!' he roared out of the window. 'How many times have I told you? No cannonballs in the lake!'

'Oops, Wing Commander! Didn't see you

there!' Peter called back as he backstroked towards the shore.

Wing Commander Oinks-Gruntington turned his soggy moustache towards Curly. 'The thing is, lad . . . I've asked you to come in today because I felt I had to meet the young pig who would go to so much effort to contact us. I think you might make a fine addition to the PiPs –'

'Really?' gasped Curly, but the Wing Commander hadn't finished.

'– one day. Maybe if you come back in a few years . . .'

Curly didn't hear the rest. After all these years, the answer was NO! He *wasn't* going to be a PiP, after all?

He felt his face burning. His ears were ringing.

No, wait — his ears weren't ringing, but a loud alarm squeal *was*. It was blasting out of the speakers all over PiPs HQ.

KWEEEEEEEEEEEEEEEEEEEEEEP!
KWEEEEEEEEEEEEEEEEEEEEEEE-EEEEEEEEEEEEEEEEEEEEEEEEEEEP!

It was the Alarm Squeal. Somewhere in Animal Paradise, there was an emergency. It was a job for the Pigs in Planes!

Lola's voice came over the speakers and echoed all around the base. 'This is a Code Pink alert! I repeat, Code Pink. PiPs, scramble!'

Down on the runway, Tammy Snuffles dropped her tools, wiped her oily trotters on her overalls, and ran towards her jet.

In the PiPs library, Brian carefully bookmarked his page and swapped his glasses for his flying helmet.

Down by Left Nostril Lake, Peter sprang out of the water and pulled his flightsuit up over his trunks. He stopped only to check in a mirror – one of the many scattered around the base for just this purpose – that his hair was looking as fine as usual. Then, with just a quick wink at his reflection, he raced for the PiPs jets too.

Meanwhile Wing Commander Oinks-Gruntington huffed and puffed into the outer office, where Lola was sitting in front of a huge radio. She had headphones on and a microphone in one trotter.

Curly just watched as the Wing Commander grabbed his helmet and raced towards the Emergency Pole down to the ground floor.

Lola covered up her mike. 'What exactly are you doing?' she asked, in the way a piglet might speak to an elderly boar who was trying to turn a computer on by hitting it again and again. 'You said you weren't going out on missions any more.'

'Nonsense!' said the Wing Commander. 'The squad needs me!'

He jumped, grabbed the pole and started to whizz down it. Unfortunately he didn't get too far. His trotters and legs made it through the hole. It was when his belly reached the gap that things got tricky.

He was stuck.

'Nice one! I *said* you should lay off the choccy bickies,' said Lola kindly.

'Stop talking and give me a shove!' ordered the Wing

Commander.

After another eye-roll, Lola pushed down on one shoulder and Curly on the other.

'Harder!'

They pushed harder.

'Too hard!' wailed the Wing Commander. He was going a bit purple now.

Next they tried pulling him back up, but this didn't work either. He was stuck like a cork in a bottle. A *big* cork, in a small bottle.

The roar of jet engines firing up outside filled the room.

'What now?' said the Wing Commander glumly. 'The team needs me.'

Lola knew. 'Let Curly here go! He can fly with Pete!'

Curly's heart did a backflip and one or two other fancy gymnastic moves. Was he going to get a chance after all?

The Wing Commander's moustache looked whiter than ever against the darkening purple of his chops. 'Impossible! He's hardly more than a piglet. And only fully trained PiPs are allowed on missions!'

He looked down angrily. 'Why hasn't anyone made this hole wider?'

'It was against the rules,' Lola answered coolly. '*Your* rules, to be precise.'

The Wing Commander's moustache twitched. 'Very well,' he grumbled. 'You can go on this one mission, McHoglet.'

'Brill!' cried Curly, and then he was charging down the stairs and out to the runway with a great big grin from pig's ear to pig's ear.

From the lead jet's cockpit, Peter Porker watched the young pig racing his way.

'What's the kid doing?' he asked into his mike.

'His name's Curly,' answered Lola over the radio. 'He's taking Peregrine's place on this mission. He'll fly with you.'

Pete grinned. 'Where's the Wing Commander then? At the shops because he ran out of biscuits?'

'I heard that, Porker!' came the Wing Commander's strained voice over the radio.

As Curly climbed up into the cockpit behind him, Pete nodded hello. 'Strap in tight, kid. This might be a bumpy ride.'

'Don't worry about me, Captain Porker,' said Curly, trying to sound cool. 'I've flown loads of times.'

Pete looked back at the other two jets. Brian gave him the thumbs-up. As usual, his plane shone and sparkled because he'd spent ages cleaning and polishing it.

Over on the other side, Tammy's plane was a different kettle of fish (which is a bit what it smelled like). It was so mucky you couldn't tell what colour it was under the grime. The other PiPs called her plane the 'Sty in the Sky'. Instead of a thumbs-up, she waved a half-eaten cheese sandwich she'd found on the control panel.

A thrill of excitement ran down Curly's back all the way to his curly tail. Here he was, inside a real PiPs jet, about to go on a mission!

'PiPs, you are cleared for take-off,' announced Lola.

'Three . . .' Pete gave the control dials a final check.

'Two . . .' The engine noise was louder than ever.

'One . . .' Pete popped on the special mirror sunglasses he always wore on missions.

'PiPs are GO!'

CHAPTER 2:

The Eggs Factor

The engines screamed as the jet zoomed up, up, up. G-force slammed Curly back into his seat.

'You OK back there, kid?' Pete asked.

'WAAAH!' replied Curly. He *had* flown loads of times, but never like this!

'PiP 1 is airborne,' Pete said into his radio. 'Hogs are high in the sky!'

'Copy that, PiP 1,' came Lola's reply.

The jet levelled off above the clouds. Curly was able now to look around and see the other two planes close behind them. The three SkyHog jets were flying in a classic V formation.

Fluffy clouds were spread out below but there was no time to admire the view. Lola was telling them their map coordinates over the radio.

'I know that place,' said Pete, as he banked east. 'That's Chicken Island, isn't it?'

'Roger,' said Lola.

'Who's Roger when he's at home?' asked Pete. He turned and winked at Curly.

'Very funny,' replied Lola, but then another voice cut in angrily.

'You know we say ROGER over the radio!' barked the Wing Commander. He was still stuck in the Emergency Pole hole, but he could hear all of the pilots on Lola's radio. 'That's the rule! Do you understand, Porker?'

'Derek!' answered Pete. 'No – Kevin! I mean, Roger, Wing Commander!'

While the Wing Commander spluttered

some more, Tammy's voice came over the radio from her plane: 'So what's the problem on Chicken Island, Lola?'

'The alarm call came from the Free-Range Happy Hatchery. That's where all of the island's eggs are hatched. They've just had a break-in and a big robbery.'

'What was taken?' asked Brian from his jet. 'Money? Jewels? Computers?'

'Eggs,' said Lola.

'*Eggs?*' asked Brian.

'Eggs-actly,' said Lola. 'Someone has nicked loads of eggs from the hatchery.'

'Why?' asked Brian.

'Maybe they want to make the world's biggest omelette?' suggested Pete. 'We'll soon know. We're almost there! Over and out!'

As they swooped below cloud level, Curly peered excitedly through the side window. He could see waves below, and something else – an island shaped like a chicken

drumstick. Chicken Island!

The three jets turned and headed to the north of the island. Down below, the buildings of Chicken Island looked like toys; the chickens of Chicken Island looked like ants; the ants of Chicken Island . . . well, Curly couldn't see *them* at all.

At last they spotted the Free-Range Happy Hatchery.

Pete flew lower and did a fly-by. 'There's nowhere long and flat enough for a normal landing,' he radioed the other pilots. 'We'll have to make a vertical landing in that field.'

'Affirmative,' answered Brian.

'No probs,' said Tammy.

Curly watched as Pete engaged the retro-jets. 'Wow!' he gasped.

'These SkyHog P-11s are top of the line!' grinned Pete over his shoulder. 'You could land one on a postage stamp if you wanted, although you might not be able to use it on a postcard afterwards.' The plane started to zoom straight down, like a wobbly lift.

Moments later all three jets were on the ground. As the cockpits popped open and the PiPs climbed down, a large hen in a white uniform ran out to meet them.

'Hello there,' said Pete, smoothing back his hair and giving his most charming smile. 'I'm Captain Peter Porker of the PiPs fleet. Happy to be of service.'

Brian and Tammy looked at each other and rolled their eyes with amusement.

'I'm Matron Peck,' the hen said in a no-nonsense cluck. 'But let's get to the point. There's no time to lose!'

'Oh, OK,' said Pete, slightly surprised. 'Well, erm, how can we help?'

Behind the matron lots of other chickens were running around in a panic, flapping their wings and clucking and squawking.

'What's up with that lot?' asked Tammy. 'They're running around like headless chickens.'

Matron Peck glared with unblinking yellow eyes.

'Oops, sorry,' said Tammy. 'Didn't mean to ruffle your . . . er . . . feathers.'

Matron Peck still hadn't blinked.

'I'll just stop talking now,' Tammy mumbled.

'Most of the chickens are running to the laying area,' said Matron Peck coldly.

'Chickens often lay when they get scared,' explained Brian.

Curly knew that Brian 'the Brain' Trotter was a highly intelligent pig. He'd been top of his class in the best medical school on Pig Island. He was a vital member of the PiPs because he knew almost everything about all the species of Animal Paradise.

'Why are they all scared?' Pete started to ask, but then he remembered that his fly-by *had* been quite low. 'Oh . . . Oops, sorry.'

Matron Peck shook her head. 'Walk this way,' she said sharply. She turned and trotted off towards the nearest building.

The four pigs followed the large hen, Tammy trying desperately *not* to 'walk this way', that is, like a chicken. Inside, the building was dimly lit, but they could see dozens and dozens of eggs, all lined up in neat little rows. On the walls there were posters showing pictures of pretty farmyards and slogans like '*Coop, Sweet Coop*'.

The place would have felt nice and cosy, except there were heating bars set into the low ceilings and it was very hot.

'We'll be streaky rashers if we're in here too long,' gasped Curly.

'The incubator rooms must be hot at all times,' said Matron Peck, leading the pigs between the rows. 'These are just a few days old.'

Brian recognized the gentle classical music playing quietly in the background. 'That's the "Ode to Freedom" by my favourite composer, Wolfgang Hamadeus Mozart,' he said. 'I think it's the Pig Island Porkestra playing.'

Matron Peck gave a stiff nod. 'Here at the Free-Range Happy Hatchery we play classical music to our unhatched eggs – Mozart, Beethoofen, Cluckmaninov. We believe it helps to create happy, healthy chickens who grow up to do the right thing.' She fluffed her feathers. 'Chicken Island is a happy, peaceful place. I have no idea who would want to change that by stealing our eggs.' Sighing, she held open the door into the next hall. 'Come on,' she told the pigs, '"quick as a chick", as I like to tell the hatchlings!'

They passed through to another room where the eggs were about a week old. As they walked through each hall, the eggs were a little older than those in the room before.

As they carried on, Brian asked, 'I've often wondered . . . Which came first, the chicken or the egg?'

'That's easy,' said Tammy. 'It's the chicken.

You can't have an egg without a chicken to lay it!'

'I think it's the egg,' Curly piped up. 'You can't have a chicken that hasn't hatched from an egg, can you?'

Pete stayed silent. He was more a pig of action than a deep thinker. The last question like this he'd pondered was, 'Which came first, the hair gel or the hairspray?'

Matron Peck had reached one last door. She rested a sturdy wing on the handle before going in. 'This is the final incubator room,' she said grimly.

They followed her in.

'As you can see, it's very different from the others,' said the matron.

Pete nodded, looking around. 'You bet! The walls are a slightly different shade of cream, aren't they?'

Matron Peck's yellow eyes just blinked.

'Erm, I think she's talking about the eggs,

not the decorating,' said Curly. 'As in: there aren't any in here.'

It was true. Like all the other incubator rooms, this one had dozens of rows of little holes for the eggs to sit in. But *unlike* the other incubator rooms, all of the little holes were empty. The eggs were gone!

Tammy was looking around. 'There's something else different, as well,' she said. 'It's colder in here. I can feel a draught!'

It wasn't hard to see why. One of the wooden shutters on the wall was open a little.

Curly opened the shutter wider and was leaning out.

'Those should always be kept shut!' clucked Matron Peck.

'But there are footprints here!' the piglet cried. 'Lots of them!'

Brian knew the *Encyclopedia of Animal Tracks* off by heart. He peered down at the footprints on the ground outside. There were several pairs of them.

'Those are definitely chicken footprints,' he said. He looked up at the other PiPs with a grave expression. 'But they're the biggest ones I've ever seen in my life!'

CHAPTER 3:

Hambush!

The PiPs left Matron Peck to look after her hens and followed the chicken footprints over a wooden fence round the back of the hatchery. They continued through a meadow until they reached a road.

Brian studied the patterns on the tarmac – these weren't animal tracks, they were wide rubber tyre marks.

'It looks as though the egg-nappers loaded their haul into the back of a truck and drove off,' he said.

'But some of the chickens must have crossed the road,' said Tammy, pointing to several footprints that led away from the tyre tracks.

Pete nodded. 'The question is ... *why*? Why *did* the chickens cross the road?' With Peregrine back at base, it was his job as mission leader to come up with a plan. 'Curly and I will follow these footprints and see what we find,' he said. 'Tammy, you take your plane up. See what you can see from above. Radio us if there's anything out of the ordinary.'

'Okey-dokey, Pete,' said Tammy, starting back towards the planes.

'Brian, you go with her,' added Pete.

Brian didn't budge. 'Er, maybe I should stay with you, Pete? In case there's a medical emergency,' he said. 'Perhaps Curly here can go in the Sty.'

Pete shook his head. 'The kid sticks with me.'

Brian leaned forward and whispered. 'The thing is ... This is my neatest flightsuit and I've just got it back from the dry-cleaner's. And, well . . . Tammy's plane *is* a bit messy.'

Pete looked over Brian's shoulder at Tammy, who was pulling a lump of pre-chewed bubblegum from her pocket. She brushed it off and popped it in her mouth.

'Sorry, Bri,' smiled Pete. 'Just check the seat carefully before you sit down. Chocolate stains can be hard to get out.'

As Tammy and a glum-looking Brian made their way back to the planes, Pete and Curly turned their attention to the trail of footprints along the ground.

'Let's see where these take us,' said Pete.

Where the footprints took them was up a hill. This was more exercise than either pig had taken in some time, and both were gasping for air.

'At least . . .' panted Pete, 'we know we're . . . going in the . . . right direction!'

Curly nodded – all they had to do was follow those footprints all the way to the egg-snatchers. There was just one little problem – at the top of the hill the footprints fanned out and then . . . disappeared!

'That's odd,' Pete murmured, stroking his chin.

'We'd better radio for help,' said Curly. He patted a well-thumbed copy of the *PiPs Rules and Regulations* in his pocket. Curly had carried this everywhere since he was a tiny piglet. He had even made his mother read to him from it at bedtime. 'According to the PiPs rules, operatives have to radio in anything unusual.'

Pete put a trotter on Curly's shoulder. 'I didn't say it was "unusual", did I? Just *odd*.'

Curly was puzzled. 'Um . . . that's the same thing, isn't it? And according to the rules –'

Pete treated the young pig to his dazzling grin. 'I'll tell you something about rules, kid,' he said. 'They're a bit like eggs.'

'What, you boil them for four and a half minutes?'

'No . . . you have to break them when you're making a cake.'

'We're not making a cake,' said Curly, even more puzzled. 'We're investigating a crime.'

But Pete had already started down the other side of the hill towards the thicket of trees below. 'Look at it this way, kid. Sometimes you just have to trust your gut instincts. And right now my gut is telling me to head towards those trees. Then we'll radio in what we find. OK?'

'OK,' said Curly uncertainly, as he too set off down the hill after his hero and his hero's hero-sized gut.

Up in the air, Tammy and Brian were circling the surrounding area in Tammy's plane, the Sty in the Sky. (They would have been up there a bit quicker but Brian had insisted on carefully spreading a few tissues over his seat.) So far they hadn't spotted anything suspicious. They weren't able to see the roads below because this part of the island was covered by woods.

'If only we had some kind of on-board heat sensor,' said Brian.

'Why's that?'

'You know how hot it was back there in the incubator rooms?' asked Brian. 'Well, if the egg-nappers are going to hatch those eggs, they'll have to use a lot of heat.'

Tammy grinned. 'Press that red button, will you, Bri?' she said. 'I think it's under the empty pizza box.'

Brian looked around gloomily. 'No, it isn't.' He sighed. 'It's under this *pizza*.'

'Ooh, I wondered where I'd put that!' said Tammy. 'Pass me a slice!'

'What does the red button do anyway?' asked Brian, while Tammy munched.

She tossed the pizza crust over her shoulder. 'Oops, sorry!' she said as it bounced off Brian's forehead. 'The red button turns the new heat sensors on. I installed them last week!'

Tammy's skills as a mechanic meant she was always upgrading her SkyHog jet with the latest experimental gizmos and machines.

'Fantastic!' Brian looked down at the new screen Tammy had bolted on to the side of the cockpit. Everything looked green and blue on it, apart from one big patch of red behind them.

'That's the Free-Range Happy Hatchery,' said Tammy. 'What about ahead of us?'

Brian checked. 'There's another big patch of red to the south-east – something over there is giving off loads of heat.'

Tammy grinned. 'So that's where we're going!'

'OK, sounds great,' said Brian. *And wherever it is, I hope they'll have some soap*, he thought.

Pete and Curly could hear the drone of Tammy's plane growing fainter overhead.

'They must have spotted something,' said Pete, as they approached the thicket of trees.

'Shall we call them and check?' asked Curly. He looked nervously at the trees looming up ahead. It felt like someone or something was watching their every move.

But Pete's attention was focused on something on the ground ahead of them. A little red feather was standing, point down in the earth, fluttering in the breeze.

'It's a clue!' said Pete, running towards the feather.

Curly didn't answer. He couldn't shake the feeling that they were being watched . . . by several pairs of beady yellow eyes. He looked at the dark trees all around them, and a nasty little thought crawled into his mind.

'Er, Pete?' he began. 'What if this isn't a clue?'

'What else could it be?' asked Pete.

'Well . . .' Curly gulped. 'What if it's a *trap*?'

Several dark shapes seemed to move in the lower branches.

'Don't worry, kid!' said Pete. 'I'm a professional and my gut tells me –'

'Now!' barked a deep voice, and then five figures swooped down to the ground from their hiding-places in the trees. They were roosters, but no ordinary roosters – dressed in combat jackets, these were bigger and tougher-looking than any either pig had ever seen.

Fear froze Curly to the spot, but Pete stepped forward. He didn't seem worried –

after all, these roosters might look tough *for chickens*, but they were still just chickens. *He* was a big, strong pig, trained by the most elite crime-fighting unit in Animal Paradise.

Suddenly there was a loud growling sound.

Pete looked down and spoke to his belly. 'Hmm, I guess that "gut feeling" was just you wanting lunch!'

The heat was coming from a large, flat-roofed building. Tammy didn't want to land the Sty too near to it, so she touched down about half a kilometre away, behind a line of trees. She and Brian spent a few minutes making sure the plane wasn't visible from the road.

'I don't think anyone will see that,' said Tammy.

'They might smell it,' muttered Brian under his breath.

They set out towards the building. It wasn't long before they heard the sound of an engine behind them. Something was coming!

'Quick! Get under that bush!' Tammy cried. 'Hit the dirt!'

Brian didn't like this idea much, especially the bit about 'dirt'. After all, he had spent precisely forty-seven minutes that morning ironing nice sharp creases into his flightsuit. He didn't want to get it all mucky now!

So, while Tammy dived into the mud, Brian lowered himself carefully on to a patch of dry grass. He was just in time. Moments later, an army truck with a canvas back drove past.

The two pigs peeked out. 'It's heading towards the building,' said Tammy.

She was rummaging in her huge rucksack.

'What have you got in there?' asked Brian.

'Just a few bits and bobs,' answered Tammy. 'A tube of suncream, a postcard of Donkey Island, some emergency dried water, an inflatable raft, washing-up liquid, a pair of flippers, a snack in case we get hungry, and . . .' She pulled out a pair of binoculars. 'These!'

She put the binoculars to her eyes and

pointed them at the back of the truck.

'What can you see?' asked Brian.

'I'm not sure. It's all weird and brown and blobby,' Tammy said. 'Oh no, wait a minute . . .' She peeled a half-chewed toffee from one of the lenses, then looked again. 'That's better. I can see a few roosters. Wow, they're big! And I can see boxes of eggs. Lots and lots of eggs!'

CHAPTER 4:

Rooster Booster

To get as close as possible to the big building without being seen, Brian and Tammy followed a ditch that ran alongside the road. Brian took his time because he didn't want his brand-new, all-weather boots to get wet.

Tammy looked through her binoculars again. 'The building's set back behind a big barbed-wire fence. I can see an entrance gate, but it's got two rooster guards.'

As they got closer, they realized just how high the fence around the building was. It was topped off with barbed wire and it was giving off a low buzzing sound.

'That fence is electrified,' said Brian glumly. 'If we try to climb over we'll get frazzled to pork scratchings!'

'Then how are we going to get in?' asked Tammy. 'It's not as if another truck is just going to roll up and stop at the gate, so we can jump in the back and ride in, is it?'

Brian hesitated because, just at that moment, another truck was rolling up and stopping at the gate. As before, the guards were questioning the chicken behind the wheel.

'Quick! This is our only chance!' hissed Tammy.

'Er . . .'

Brian wasn't so sure. This second truck wasn't an army truck like the last one; it was a rubbish truck! The thought of riding in the back of a rubbish truck, on top of piles and piles of smelly, slimy rubbish, was enough to uncurl Brian's tail with horror.

'Wait! Maybe we *should* try the fence?' he said. 'It isn't SO high. Have you got a rocket-powered pogo stick in that backpack of yours?'

Tammy didn't answer. She jumped out of the ditch and ran towards the truck, making sure that neither the driver nor the two rooster guards could see her.

Brian held back, but then the truck revved its engine. It was now or never. With a deep sigh, Brian scurried forward.

Tammy was already in the back of the truck. She made a frantic one-trotter gesture for Brian to get a move on. The truck was starting to roll forward towards the gate.

Brian sped up. It wasn't easy to jump into the back of the rubbish truck while holding a white hanky over his snout, but somehow he managed it. He prepared himself for the horrible stink of old rubbish to fill his nostrils. But it didn't — the back of the

rubbish truck was clean and shiny.

'It's your lucky day, Bri,' grinned Tammy. 'The truck has just been cleaned. This place must be its first stop today.'

The pigs heard the gate being rolled back, and they ducked down as the truck passed the two guards. They were inside. Whatever the roosters were up to, these two PiPs had a chance of finding out!

★ ★ ★

As Pete's stomach finished rumbling, he took another step towards the gang of roosters. *What harm could a few chickens do to a pig like him?* he thought.

'Bring it on,' he challenged.

The biggest rooster gave a little nod. It must have been a command, because a moment later one of the other chickens put its head down and charged Pete. It hit him like a feathered missile and slammed him back into a tree trunk.

'*OOF!*'

Pete got back up to his feet and put on a determined smile. 'Want to play rough, do you? OK – let's try that again.'

He moved into a wide-legged stance with one front-trotter straight out and the other curled high over his head. 'And before you birdbrains do something you might regret, I should tell you . . . I'm a black belt in the ancient piggy fighting art of Kung Poo. And trust me, you do *not* want to get in the way of my Kung Poo pork chop to the neck!'

The confidence in his hero's voice set Curly's mind at rest a little. He watched as Pete began to whirlwind his short fat pink arms in the air, all the while hopping up and down and letting out cries of '*Hi-YAH! YAH!*'

He flung out his legs in higher and higher Kung Poo kicks. Then he got carried away, kicked too high and lost his footing. He flipped up into the air and landed on his rear end.

'*Hi-OW!*'

'Get the fat fool!' crowed the biggest rooster.

'Oi, who are you calling fat?' demanded Pete as the four roosters charged him.

Curly couldn't believe his eyes. Pete had failed! Now the sight of four huge roosters jumping on top of his hero snapped him into action.

Curly spun around and started legging it back up the hill.

'Run like the wind, kid!' shouted Pete after him. Of course, there wasn't much chance of this – Curly was a pig, after all – but he did run like a very fast pig.

The biggest rooster shouted out, 'Stop him!' and Curly expected to hear the sound of rapid footsteps behind him. But he didn't hear anything. Was no one following him?

He risked a quick glance around over his shoulder. There was no sound of footsteps

because two of the roosters were *flying* after
him, swooping through the air like birds of
prey. They whizzed closer and closer, and
then landed . . . right on top of him.

BOOF!

There was nothing Curly could do as
strong wings yanked him to his feet. One of
the chickens tied his trotters behind his back.

As they began to lead him back towards
the trees, Curly understood now why the

trail of footprints had ended at the top of the hill. The chickens making them had *flown* down the hill! But how was that possible?

'Chickens can't fly,' Curly said. 'Not like *that*.'

'We can now,' said one of the chickens darkly.

The rubbish truck slowed as it neared a line of bins. Tammy and Brian seized the chance to hop out and scurry round a corner.

They could see now that the large shed they'd first spotted was just one of many buildings.

'It looks like some kind of top-secret military base,' said Tammy.

'What makes you say that?' asked Brian, who was busy polishing his glasses.

Tammy just pointed at a wooden sign that read:

MILITARY BASE

TOP SECRET

'Oh, I see,' said Brian, putting his glasses back on.

The army truck they had seen earlier was parked alongside a side door in the big building. It was empty now.

'Bet the eggs are inside,' said Tammy.

Brian turned his head. 'What's that sound?'

They could hear a rooster crowing orders and the drum of marching chicken feet. The noise got louder and louder. They were coming towards them.

The two PiPs froze. Should they jump into the back of the truck? Run back to the gate? There was no time!

'Let's try the building,' suggested Brian.

They raced past the empty truck and Tammy pushed on the door with her trotter. 'It's open!' she cried.

They scrambled in and pushed the door almost closed. Through the thin gap they saw a troop of chickens march past seconds later.

'Yikes,' said Tammy, pushing the door firmly shut with a click. 'Something's definitely not right here.'

The pigs turned round and saw that they were inside a huge low room. Its purpose was clear: this was another hatchery.

'So this is where the eggs went,' said Tammy.

The eggs were set in long rows under heaters, but in every other way this place was very different from the Free-Range Happy Hatchery. There was no soft tinkle of classical music, only the low drone of the heating system. There were no windows, no pictures on the walls of happy hens, no signs saying: 'Happy Eggs Come from Happy Chickens' or 'A Chick is for

Life, not just for Easter'.

'I'm going to call Pete and tell him where we are,' said Tammy, reaching for her radio. But as soon as she tried to alert the captain she groaned. 'There's no reception in here. We'll just have to wait until we get outside again.'

But Brian was distracted. 'These eggs are going to hatch soon,' he said, examining the rows. 'So what would the Chicken Army want with so many new hatchlings?'

Before Tammy could answer, the door handle turned. The two pigs ducked behind a stack of empty cardboard boxes and peeked round the sides as a chicken came into the room. At least, they *thought* it was a chicken. It was hard to tell because it was wearing a beak-mask and industrial safety goggles.

The chicken tore open a cardboard box on the other side of the room and took out a plastic canister full of green liquid. It slotted the canister into some sort of spray-gun. Then it walked up and down the rows of eggs, spraying all of them with the liquid. As the tiny droplets filled the air, Brian, who was allergic to a long list of things, had to fight the urge to sneeze.

At last, the chicken kicked the empty box over to the other side of the room, close to the pigs' hiding-place. Then the chicken left the same way it had come in.

'What was it spraying on to the eggs?'

asked Brian. He looked at one of the cardboard boxes. Two words were printed on the side: ROOSTER BOOSTER.

'What's *that*?' he murmured.

But Tammy had other things on her mind. She rushed over to the door, past the rows of sprayed green eggs. She started pulling it

with all her strength.

'We've got another problem,' she said. 'When it left, that chicken locked the door. We're stuck in here!'

CHAPTER 5:

Green Eggs and Cheese and Ham

Curly didn't want to admit it, but he was scared. He and Pete were prisoners! They were in handcuffs, surrounded by oversized chickens and bumping up and down in the back of an army jeep.

The leader of the roosters was glaring at Pete. 'Why were you following us, pig?'

Pete just smiled. 'I've already told you all I'm going to say – my name, my rank and how many sugars I like in my tea. Eight, if you wouldn't mind.'

The big rooster turned his attention to Curly. 'You – what are you doing here on

Chicken Island?'

Curly gulped. 'Well . . .'

'Leave the kid alone,' Pete said. 'He just came along for the ride.'

'It doesn't matter,' sneered the rooster. 'Colonel Cluck will find out everything he needs to know. He can be very . . . *persuasive*.'

A shiver sprinted down Curly's spine.

They rode on in silence. Finally the jeep slowed down as it passed a sentry-box. The guard on duty waved them through into a big military base. There were rows of barracks, and hangars full of planes and tanks. Curly could see a squad of marching chickens trooping up and down.

The big rooster looked up as they drove past a large clock. 'Time for a dose of Booster, lads,' he said to the rest of his squad.

All of the chickens pulled little flasks out of their combat jackets and began to pour a green liquid down their beaks.

'Ooh, I like fizzy pop too!' said Pete. 'Can
I have a swig?'

'This isn't for mammals,' said one rooster.
'Just chickens.' All of the non-pigs in the
truck began to laugh.

'Hur, hur, hur.'

This wasn't the kind of laugh you hear
when animals are playing happily in the
park. It was more the kind of dark laugh
that makes you very, very nervous that
something terrible is on the way.

With no way out of the darkened incubator
room and no radio signal, all Tammy and
Brian could do was sit and wait until
someone opened the door again.

'I spy, with my piggy eye, something beginning with E,' said Tammy.

Brian looked at the hundreds of sinister green eggs all around them and sighed. They listened to the buzz of the incubator room's heaters for a while. Soon Brian realized that he could hear another sound too.

'What's that?' he asked. 'Sounds like something being lowered into a vat of toxic waste.'

'It's my tummy rumbling,' said Tammy. 'It always does that if I skip a meal.' She began looking in her backpack. 'We may as well have a bite to eat.'

Actually, Brian had to admit he was also

feeling peckish. Maybe a little light lunch was a sensible idea.

'Have you got any carrot sticks?' he asked. 'Or low-fat, salt-free rice cakes?'

Tammy pulled out several packs of neon-yellow cheese slices and slapped them down. 'I've got cheese!' she said. 'Loads actually — it was on special at the supermarket.'

Brian wrinkled his snout. 'I do not care for cheese.'

'What?' said Tammy, unwrapping a bright yellow slice and shoving it into her mouth. 'Who doesn't like cheese?'

'Me,' sniffed Brian.

Tammy couldn't believe her ears. 'So you're telling me you don't like cheese on toast?'

'I do not.'

'*Weird!* What about cheese and onion crisps?'

'Absolutely not.'

Tammy munched another slice, swallowed and burped, then asked, 'Baked potato with beans and cheese?'

'Never.'

Tammy thought long and hard. 'What about Strawberry Surprise?'

Brian unwrinkled his snout a little. 'That sounds OK.'

Tammy smiled and reached into her bag. 'Close your eyes and try this Strawberry Surprise then.' She popped something into Brian's mouth.

He swallowed and then pulled a face. 'Ugh! What's in it?'

'Just cheese!' grinned Tammy. 'That's the surprise!'

Meanwhile back at PiPs HQ on Pig Island, Wing Commander Peregrine Oinks-Gruntington was still stuck fast halfway down the Emergency Pole. Lola was staring with concern at the new colour of his face.

'That reminds me,' she said, popping a piece of bubblegum into her mouth. 'I must buy a pair of those bright purple trousers at Top Hog. They glow in the dark, you know?'

'Forget shopping!' exclaimed the Wing Commander. 'Help me out of here!'

Lola blew a big pink, faintly Wing-Commanderish bubble. 'I could always try and cut you out with a chainsaw.'

Peregrine had seen how Lola opened envelopes with scissors; who knew what harm she might do with a chainsaw? 'No!' he cried.

'OK . . . why don't I just call the Fire Brigade?'

This idea sounded even worse to Peregrine. 'I'd be the laughing-stock of Pig Island,' he moaned. 'Any other bright ideas?'

Lola perked up. 'I could always film

you on my phone and send it to *You've Made a Right Pig's Ear of That!* on TV. They pay £100 for every clip of some pig in an embarrassing situation. That would more than pay for a few pairs of those trousers and I'd finally be famous!'

'Out of the question!' huffed Peregrine.

Lola shrugged. 'No probs. We'll just have to wait until you've lost some weight around your belly then.' She flicked open the new copy of *Sizzle!* magazine on her desk. 'It should only take a couple of days, but don't worry – I'll make sure you aren't bored while I check in with the team. You can read this article about hunky Hollywood hog, Brad Pigg.'

Peregrine rolled his eyes in despair.

★ ★ ★

A fresh chicken was waiting to meet the jeep.

'Colonel Cluck will see the prisoners now,' he announced.

Pete and Curly clambered out and the new rooster led them through the base. He was very different from the other chickens. For one thing, he was normal-sized, but he also seemed a lot friendlier. At least, he introduced himself – he said his name was Nugget – and he said, 'Follow me, please,' which was a big improvement on 'Follow me, stupid pigs!'

They went past a platoon of chickens who were standing to attention while a rooster officer inspected them.

As Pete slowed down to watch, Nugget looked back and said, 'Hurry up, please –

quick as a chick! It isn't a good idea to keep
Colonel Cluck waiting.'

'I'll tell you something, Nugget,' Pete said.
'Captain Peter Porker is worth waiting for!
Now, any chance you could undo these
cuffs? I'd hate them to leave marks on my
nice soft skin.'

Nugget just raised an eyebrow.

'You don't seem much like the other
chickens here,' Curly said to their guide.

Nugget said nothing, but he looked as if
he was biting his beak not to answer.

'Is it something to do with that booster
drink?' asked Pete. 'Is that why they're all so
big and tough?'

Nugget hesitated, then gave a little nod.
He looked around nervously to make sure
no one could hear them. Then he whispered,
'It's called Rooster Booster,' he said. 'It
makes chickens bigger, stronger, faster . . .'

A pair of muscular roosters turned the

corner in front of them. 'Out of the way, Tiny!' one snarled at Nugget. 'Or you'll be eating a feather sandwich!'

Nugget stepped to the side. He was clearly bottom of the pecking order round here.

'Rooster Booster makes them more aggressive too,' he sighed when the two chickens had passed.

They were approaching a low building with two guards outside and there was just time for one last question. 'What about you, Nugget?' asked Pete. 'Don't *you* take Rooster Booster?'

'The Booster works on 999 chickens out of every thousand.' The undersized chicken gave a sad little shrug. 'It turns out I'm just the chicken in a thousand.'

There was no time to find out more. The guards shoved them through the door. Inside was some sort of army headquarters where a group of senior officer chickens was studying a big 3-D map of Chicken Island. They all turned towards the two pigs.

'Colonel Cluck will speak to you now, pigs,' the guard said gruffly.

Pete stepped forward. 'OK, I'm ready when you are,' he said. 'Where is this colonel of yours then?'

An angry voice rose from somewhere near the floor. 'Right in front of you, idiot mammal!'

Pete looked down at a fat little white-and- red rooster. He was much shorter than the other roosters there – shorter even than Nugget – but he made up for his lack of height with a gigantic red crest on top of his head.

He had an eye-patch on and his other eye blazed a fiery yellow.

'Oops, sorry,' Pete said. 'Didn't see you down there, little guy.'

For some reason this friendly comment made the little rooster even angrier. He strutted forward, his one beady eye flashing furiously.

'You will address me by my proper rank, hog!' he seethed. 'I am Colonel Harlan J. Cluck of the Fifth Bantam Division of the glorious Chicken Army.'

'OK, keep your feathers on, Clucky,' said Pete.

Colonel Cluck glared at him. 'Tell us why you are here,' he demanded.

Curly expected Pete to say something about the missing eggs, but instead the captain said, 'We want to know more about this amazing Rooster Booster of yours.'

'I knew it!' crowed Colonel Cluck. 'Every

creature in Animal Paradise wants to get its paws or claws on the Rooster Booster formula. But only I know the secret recipe!'

Pete grinned.

'Soon we will wipe that smirk off your snout, you big, stupid, ugly mammal!' snapped Cluck.

'Let me get this straight – *you're* calling *me* ugly?' Pete replied. 'You ought to have a peek in the mirror, pal. That power-mad rooster look is *so* last year.'

Curly wished Pete would be quiet. Their situation was bad enough without making the rooster even madder. But then he heard the distant sound of a plane and his heart leapt.

Colonel Cluck had heard it too. He was at the window now. When he spoke again, his voice was syrupy. 'Do you recognize that sound?' he asked, pointing a wing up to the sky.

'I'd know that sound anywhere,' Curly said with a nod. 'It's a PiPs jet.' Even though he was still afraid, he was starting to feel hopeful. 'That'll be the other members of our team. They're probably flying off to get help right now. You can't keep us prisoners!'

But Pete didn't join in. The sound of the plane was getting louder now. Seconds later it appeared over the Chicken Army base.

Curly frowned. 'What are they doing?' he asked. 'Why aren't they going for help?'

Pete spoke at last. 'That isn't Tammy's plane. It's mine.'

The plane did a wide loop and then landed on the runway outside the window. To his horror, Curly saw the pilot get out and remove his flying helmet. It was a chicken!

'I told my troops to recover your plane from near the hatchery,' explained Colonel Cluck. 'They found the other plane too.

Which just leaves one question . . . If they're not with the jet, where *are* your fellow PiPs?'

Peter Porker said nothing.

'Allow me to put you out of your misery,' said Cluck. He clapped his wings together and ordered one of the guards to click on a TV screen in the corner of the room.

'Go to camera fourteen,' Cluck ordered.

The picture on the screen showed a dark room full of eggs. Curly felt sure that those were the eggs that had gone missing from the hatchery. But there was something else in the room – two large pale shapes. It was Tammy and Brian!

'I should have mentioned it earlier,' smirked Cluck. 'Our cameras have been tracking your two friends ever since they illegally entered our base. They're locked in the incubator shed right now.' He sighed with fake concern. 'I'm afraid things are going to get rather ... *unpleasant* for them in there. Quite *deadly*, in fact.'

Curly's heart sank. If the other PiPs were prisoners too, how was anyone going to help them now?

CHAPTER 6:

Generation Eggs

Tammy and Brian were still cooped up.
Tammy gave one final gigantic burp to
signal that she had finished snacking on
cheese.

Brian tried to smile politely and failed.
Then he cocked his head to one side – now
Tammy had stopped slurping, he could hear
something else – a faint tap-tap-tapping.

'What's that?'

'I can hear it too!' said Tammy. 'It's
coming from one of the eggs.'

It took them a while to identify which
one was making the sound.

'This one!' said Brian at last.

The two pigs listened as the tapping got faster. Finally a thin crack appeared in the egg's shell. Another one joined it, then another. The network of cracks spread until finally there was a little hole in the side of the egg. A chick was getting ready to come out!

'Ooh, I can see its little beak!' exclaimed Tammy.

Soon they could see the chick's head. It continued to chip at the shell from the inside, not stopping to rest, and before long the fluffy little chick was free. It stood blinking before them with a proud little *peep*.

Brian leaned closer to the chick and beamed. 'The miracle of life always amazes me,' he began, wiping away tears of wonder. 'The look of hope in those newborn eyes as they gaze on the world for the first . . . OW!'

The chick had hopped up and jabbed at

his snout with its pointy little beak. More tears formed in Brian's eyes, but these didn't have much to do with wonder.

'It bit me!' Brian exclaimed.

'True,' Tammy said, 'but just think of the look of hope in its newborn eyes as . . . OW!'

This time the chick had sprung up and pecked Tammy.

'Oi, that hurt!' she said, grabbing the little chick. 'I'm going to keep you where I can keep an eye on you, you fluffy little punk!'

The chick began to peep angrily and stab its sharp beak at the pig's trotter.

Tammy glared at it. 'What *is* your problem?'

'Um, perhaps we should be worrying about *our* problem,' said Brian. 'Listen!'

The soft tap-tap-tapping was coming from *lots* of eggs in the room now. Hundreds of sharp little beaks were chiselling their way out. Soon a chorus of little peeps joined the tapping.

Those peeps didn't sound cute and they didn't sound sweet.

They sounded *angry*.

Pete and Curly were watching all this on the CCTV screen.

'You are witnessing a proud moment in chicken history,' Colonel Cluck told them.

They watched as more of the eggs in the incubator shed hatched. The picture wasn't good, but as far as Curly could tell, as soon as a chick hatched it launched itself at Tammy and Brian in a frenzied attack. The pigs were doing their best to knock the chicks away, but this seemed to be getting harder minute by minute.

Curly had to look away, but Pete just said, 'I'm not too keen on this programme. Could you turn over to *Pig Brother*?'

Colonel Cluck ruffled his feathers crossly. 'Still joking, eh? Then perhaps you'll find this amusing . . .' He waved a stubby wing at the CCTV screen. 'Rooster Booster works wonders on adult chickens, but that's nothing compared to the effect it has when applied to unhatched eggs. The chicks that emerge are the biggest, the fastest, the downright *meanest* chickens ever to walk the earth. They are the future of poultry, the next generation of super-chickens. They are Generation Eggs!'

Curly realized with horror why they had stolen the hatchery eggs. Cluck wanted to create his own army of super-chickens! 'So what happens when Generation Eggs chicks grow up?' he asked.

Cluck fixed the young pig with his yellow eye. 'They will be unstoppable warriors, and so we can begin our glorious plan! First we will take over Chicken Island, then all of Animal Paradise will fall.'

As usual Pete knew exactly the wrong word to say. 'Cute,' he murmured.

'CUTE!' screamed Colonel Cluck. The crest on his head flopped wildly. 'Will it be CUTE when one by one the islands of Animal Paradise fall under our iron claw? Will it be CUTE when all animals bow down to their natural master, the chicken?'

'That's awful,' Curly gasped.

'Thank you,' said Colonel Cluck. He directed his single fiery eye back at Pete.

'Where are your jokes now, Mr Comedy Pig?'

When Pete said nothing, Cluck turned to the other chickens in the room. 'Then allow me . . . WHY DID THE CHICKEN CROSS THE ROAD?' he demanded.

The assembled roosters knew what to reply, and they answered with one voice. 'TO FULFIL OUR DESTINY AND TAKE OVER THE WORLD!'

'Correct!' Colonel Cluck threw back his little head and crowed. The other roosters joined in, and the air was filled with lots of deafening cock-a-doodle-doos. It was like daybreak at the world's scariest farm.

'*COCK-A-DOODLE-DOO! COCK-A-DOODLE-DOO!*'

This went on for a few minutes. Only Nugget, the little rooster who had led them there, remained perfectly still and quiet in the background, broom in feathered hand.

When the racket died down, Pete took his trotters out of his ears and smiled weakly. 'I'll be honest, Cluckers – I've heard better punchlines.'

Things were getting nasty in the incubator shed. The rest of the chicks turned out to be just as vicious as the first. Each newly hatched chick looked around blinking for a second or two, before joining the peck-attack on the two pigs.

At first the PiPs were able to swat their attackers away, but this became harder and harder as more and more chicks hatched. Each one had a sharp little beak and a mean glint in its eyes.

The two pigs were forced back into the corner behind a makeshift wall of cardboard boxes. Waves of tweeting chicks pushed against the barrier like an angry yellow sea, pecking and jabbing away.

'*Peep! Peep! Peep! Peep! Peep!*' they cried in a way that seemed to mean, '*Attack! Attack! Attack! Attack! Attack!*'

'The cardboard isn't going to hold much longer!' cried Tammy. 'Then we're done for!'

As they struggled to hold the boxes in

place, Tammy heard a different noise in the middle of all the peeping.

'What was that?' she asked.

'Erm . . .' Brian looked embarrassed now as well as afraid.

Tammy sniffed. 'Poo-ee! Did you just –'

'No!' said Brian a bit too quickly.

'Are you sure you didn't just do a little tooter?'

'I am positive.'

'Really? Cos –'

'OK, yes! I did!' snapped Brian. 'I *told* you I don't eat cheese! It . . . gives me gas!'

'That's *all* we need!' said Tammy, waving a trotter in front of her snout.

'I hardly think this is the most important topic of conversation when we're about to get pecked to bits by tiny chickens,' said Brian.

But then both pigs became aware that the angry peeping of the chicks had died down.

One or two made puzzled little 'peep?' sounds. The front rank were no longer stabbing at the cardboard box defences. They were shuffling backwards and shaking their little fluffy heads.

'What's going on?' asked Brian.

'It's the pong! They hate it!' Tammy cried. 'Can't blame them either – no offence, Bri, but it *was* a bit of a room-clearer.'

But even as she spoke, the toxic cloud

was lifting. As it did, the chicks prepared to attack again. Their peeps grew louder. They were even angrier now.

Tammy began digging around in her backpack.

'What are you doing?' Brian asked.

'Cheese gives you gas, right?' Tammy pulled out the remaining packs of cheese slices and started to unwrap one. 'Then get eating,' she said, thrusting it at Brian. 'Eat like the wind!'

Brian looked down at the processed cheese glumly. 'You know I've got a highly sensitive snout,' he complained. 'I hate bad smells.'

But as the chicks started cheeping even louder, he took a slice of the hated yellow food and began miserably to munch.

All in all, it had been a day of big surprises for Curly, but perhaps the biggest surprise was the behaviour of Peter Porker. The PiPs captain had been Curly's hero for years, but somehow he didn't seem to be behaving all that heroically now. Instead, he seemed determined to make Colonel Cluck even madder than he already was.

'OK, tell me one thing, Clucky-boots,' Pete was saying now, 'when the super-chickens have taken over the world, what will you be doing?'

'I will be their supreme leader, of course,' declared Cluck grandly.

'Chicken Supreme, eh?' said Pete. 'So that's your plan.'

Cluck liked the ring of that. 'Yes, I will be the Chicken Supreme!'

The rooster officers began to give each other nervous glances. Curly was nervous too – why wouldn't Pete just stop making things worse?

But Pete didn't let up. 'How come you're

so dinky then?' he asked Cluck. 'Don't *you* take Rooster Booster? Are you one of the chickens it doesn't work on?'

'How dare you compare me with those weaklings!' snapped Cluck.

Curly noticed a few of the officers nudging each other. This seemed to be something they had discussed among themselves before now.

Pete carried on. 'I bet you don't take Rooster Booster, and I bet I know why.'

Curly couldn't believe what Porker did next. His trotters were still handcuffed behind his back, but he began flapping his elbows back and forth like wings.

'*BWAWK-BUK-BUK-BUCKAH!*' he cried.

'What are you doing?' asked Curly nervously. 'Stop it!'

'I'm making chicken noises,' answered Pete, still staring at Cluck. 'I'll bet that the colonel here is afraid to take the Booster. Because I think he's CHICKEN.'

It was the worst possible thing he could have said. Colonel Cluck looked like a balloon about to burst – only this balloon was filled with rage rather than helium.

'Enough!' snarled Cluck. 'If this is how you want to play, then we'll settle this in the Cockpit. Nugget, send for Mangler!'

Meanwhile, back on Snout Island, Lola was trying to contact the PiPs team on the radio. 'Come in, PiPs,' she said into the mike. 'Are you receiving? Over.'

She'd been trying for ages now, with no reply.

'I'm going to try the other radio in the control tower,' she told Peregrine.

'What about me?' asked the Wing Commander.

'I'll be right back. Don't go anywhere!'

As Lola strode towards the door, something
fell from her pocket.

'Wait, Lola,' said Peregrine. 'You've
dropped –'

He stopped when he saw what the object
was – a chocolate biscuit.

Peregrine knew that his fondness for
choccy bickies had got him into this mess in
the first place. It would be pretty stupid to
go and eat one now.

But then he considered the other side of
the argument:

IT. WAS. A. CHOCOLATE. BICKY.

You couldn't really argue with logic like
that.

And so Peregrine reached out to grab the
biscuit. He couldn't quite make it.

'Lola!' he shouted. 'Can you come back
in here for a minute?'

No answer.

Again Peregrine reached for the biscuit,

stretching and stretching until his trotter was mere centimetres from it. He was almost there. He began to rock his body back and forth.

With each forward rock, he came just a tiny bit closer. He added a sort of sideways wriggle to the movement, going faster and faster until . . .

Summoning all his energy, he was able to haul himself up and out of the hole. He was free! He could feel the blood returning to all the bits of his body it had stopped visiting. He shoved the biscuit into his mouth to celebrate.

But the good feeling didn't last long. Moments later Lola appeared in the doorway.

'It's a good thing you're free,' she observed. 'I can't contact them on the other radio either. I think maybe something has gone wrong with the mission.'

'Mm mm mmm mm–m mmm mm–m m mmm?' asked Peregrine.

'What?'

The Wing Commander swallowed, then repeated, 'Is the PiPs cargo plane ready to fly?'

'Yes. Tammy just fixed the hatch door yesterday,' Lola answered.

'Then what are we *waiting* for?' demanded the Wing Commander in a spray of crumbs. 'Looks like I'm going on this mission after all!'

CHAPTER 7:

In the Cockpit

Tammy handed Brian another square of processed cheese.

'Eat faster!' she wailed.

There was good reason to be afraid. Actually, there were hundreds of good reasons, and all of them were fluffy and yellow. The eggs had all hatched now and the sea of monster-chicks was scarier by the second.

But Brian could already feel the cheese reacting with his delicate digestive system. His tummy was making some alarming gurgles and pings.

But would it be in time? He looked up
to see more chicks rushing forward, beaks
like daggers. They were almost through
the cardboard boxes, shredding them like –
well – cardboard, but now he could feel the
pressure building inside his tummy.

'Do it!' shouted Tammy.

Brian tensed his tummy muscles.

Nothing.

He pushed again. And again.

And then –

BBBRRAAAPP!

It was a good one – which is to say, a
bad one. The attacking chicks stopped as
if they'd hit an invisible wall. A few started
coughing. Several tried to strike at the air,
but this only fanned the pong around.

'Id's workig!' cried Tammy, with one
trotter over her snout.

'Great,' said Brian glumly. *All those years
of studying, all those A*s in my exams, and for*

what? he thought to himself. *So I could end up stuffing my face with cheese and parping like an out-of-tune trombone?*

'Don't stop now!' shouted Tammy. 'Get more cheese down yer neck!'

Pete and Curly were taken outside the HQ building. The reason for this was a little bit worrying: the chicken known as Mangler wouldn't fit through the door.

They heard him approaching before they saw him. It seemed to Curly that the earth shook. And then, like a giant cloud moving across the sun, Mangler rounded the corner.

Calling him a 'chicken' was a bit like calling a tiger a 'kitty-cat'. The word didn't seem to fit. Mangler was super-sized, the biggest and toughest of all the roosters, but without an ounce of fat on his massive frame. It was all muscle. His beak was razor-sharp. The spurs on his legs looked sharp

enough to shave a flea's whiskers. His giant muscular thighs looked strong enough to crack walnuts. His wings looked thick and powerful.

There was no doubt he was one hard rooster.

Just the sight of him calmed Cluck down. He beamed like a proud parent showing off a toddler, the only difference being that *this* toddler was a barnyard killing machine. 'Mangler here is as fierce as an eagle, as strong as a rhino, as fast as a panther.'

'Sounds like one crazy mixed-up kid,' said Pete.

'He was the first chick to hatch from an egg treated with Rooster Booster,' continued Cluck. 'That makes him the very first member of Generation Eggs. One day, all chickens will be like this.'

For the first time, Curly noticed a look of worry on Pete's face, but the captain simply replied, 'OK, let's get this done. Where are the planes?'

'What do you mean?' asked Cluck.

'You said we were going to settle this in the cockpit, right?' said Pete.

Cluck's mad grin grew wider. 'I wasn't talking about the cockpit of a jet! I was talking about the COCKPIT – the chicken battle arena. You and Mangler are going to fight for the honour of your species . . . to the death!'

Peter Porker was hardly ever at a loss for words. But as this news sank in, and he looked again at the chicken-mountain that was Mangler, only one word came to his lips: 'Oh.'

In the darkened incubator room, Brian felt as if he was in a nightmare world of yellow – mad yellow chicks and disgusting yellow cheese.

He had lost count of how many pieces

of the hated food he had eaten. A gigantic lump of half-digested cheese was now rolling around his stomach like an out-of-control bowling-ball.

'I don't think I can eat any more,' he groaned.

Tammy glanced nervously at the army of peeping chicks that faced them.

'You *have* to, Brain,' she said, her trotter still clamped on her snout. 'They're flocking together to attack again. They'll tear us apart. That pong has really made them angry.'

She looked down at the single square of cheese in Brian's trotter. 'Where's the rest of it?' she asked.

Brian's eyes were watering, possibly because of the smell. 'There isn't any more,' he said quietly. 'This is the last piece.'

'Right, well, finish that and let's hope you're ready to rumble!'

★ ★ ★

The Cockpit was a circular arena dug into the ground. Pete and Curly watched grimly as Mangler took his position on the far side and started warming up.

'You'll be OK, won't you, Pete?' Curly whispered. 'You *do* actually know Kung Poo, don't you?'

'Not exactly,' Pete admitted under his breath. 'But I've watched a few movies. To be honest, I fell asleep for most of them, but it still counts, doesn't it?'

'Yes,' Curly lied. 'Yes, of course it does!'

'You're lying to make me feel better, aren't you?'

'Yes.'

Both pigs knew Pete stood about as much chance in this battle as a snow-pig in July. Mangler was going to turn him into a pile of pork products.

Pete's eyes met Curly's. 'Don't worry, kid,' he said. 'You'll know what to do when the time comes.'

What? thought Curly. *What does he mean by that?* There was nothing about being psychic in the PiPs rulebook.

But there was no time to ask because Pete had turned away and was walking to his side of the arena. He hummed a tune to himself as if he was going for a stroll.

Cluck and his senior officers were standing around the edge of the pit, ready to watch.

'Where's Nugget?' barked Cluck. 'Nugget, get the pig's handcuffs off him now.'

The little chicken scurried forward with a bunch of keys. As he fumbled to find the right one, Pete just hummed louder and louder. Curly recognized the tune. It was that piece by Wolfgang Hamadeus Mozart they'd heard at the Free-Range Happy Hatchery, the 'Ode to Freedom'.

Nugget hesitated for a moment and he

fumbled with the keys.

'Get a move on, Nugget, you wimpy little pullet!' yelled Cluck.

And then Pete's handcuffs were off and he stepped bravely down into the arena and started rolling his shoulders and doing stretches.

It was time to face the Chicken of Doom.

'Good luck, Captain!' shouted Curly.

'Let the best species win!' cried Colonel Cluck. 'Start fighting!'

The battle got off to a flying start for Pete, in that Mangler immediately picked him up and hurled him across the arena.

Things went downhill from there.

Curly didn't know too much about Kung Poo — also known as the Way of the Flying Trotter — but he was fairly sure it didn't involve getting swung around by the back legs with your head bumping up and down on the ground.

At one point Pete managed to duck
under the stab of his opponent's razor-sharp
beak and hop over the sweep of his dagger-
like spurs.

It was painful for Curly to watch, but
it was probably more painful for Pete,
especially when Mangler tried to flatten
him into a ham pizza.

Of course, Colonel Cluck was loving

it. He whooped and cheered and cried 'Cock-a-doodle-doo!' Everyone was so focused on the fight that they didn't even see Nugget creep up behind Curly.

The first Curly knew was when he heard the jingle of keys. Feathered hands moved over his trotters, and then with a soft *Click!* his handcuffs were off.

Curly glanced round. The little chicken had a wing feather over his beak. 'Shh!' he whispered. Then he pointed towards a large building across the field. 'That's the incubator shed over there. I don't think your friends can last much longer.' He held up his keys and pointed to the shed's door.

As he slipped away, Curly took one look back at the arena where Mangler was doing his best to bend Pete in ways pigs really weren't designed to bend. For just a second, Pete looked over at Curly and he winked at the young pig. Then he returned to the fight with renewed strength.

That's when Curly knew for sure – Pete *was* a true hero. All this time, Pete hadn't been putting his back-trotter in his mouth by accident. No, he had been *trying* to make Colonel Cluck mad. He had wanted to create a big fight so that everyone would be distracted. Now that he saw Curly was free, he was battling harder than ever so all the spectators would keep their eyes on the fight.

Inside the arena, Pete managed to free himself and get to his trotters. His eyes locked with Mangler's.

'OK then,' Pete drawled. 'No more Mr Nice Pig.'

He ran forward, fists windmilling. Mangler sidestepped and thrust a wing out. Pete ran straight into it, brilliantly striking the rooster's fist with his own chin.

And then he was lying flat on his back,
and it was beginning to look as if this
fight was over.

CHAPTER 8:

The Great Egg-splosion

Lying on his back in the centre of the Cockpit, Pete was helpless. He ached from the tip of his snout to his little tail – so curly because he put it in curlers every night. His ribs ached; his *spare ribs* ached. He was a beaten pig.

Come on, kid, he thought to himself, willing Curly to free Tammy and Brian so they could help him. *I won't be able to distract this crowd for much longer.*

Mangler stood over him, blocking the sun. He looked over towards Colonel Cluck, waiting for his orders.

The fat little rooster held his wing straight out. Pete understood what this meant – his life hung in the balance.

Then with a nasty grin Colonel Cluck turned his wing-tip feather downwards. The meaning was clear: Cluck had chosen not to spare him.

Cluck's officers didn't look happy about this. 'I don't think you can do that, Colonel,' began one.

'You aren't here to THINK!' bellowed Cluck. 'You're just muscle. I'm the brains! *I'll* do all the thinking from now on. I am the Chicken Supreme, and the Chicken Supreme says the pig must die!'

'Listen to him,' said Pete, addressing the other chickens. 'That's why he won't take Booster!'

Colonel Cluck's rage had taken him far past the point of thinking before he spoke. 'Why should I rot my brain with Rooster

Booster? The Chicken Supreme must remain clear-headed!'

The officer roosters really weren't looking happy now, but Cluck ignored them and shouted his order straight to Mangler.

'Now kill that pig!'

Mangler nodded once and extended his gigantic wings as Pete closed his eyes and prepared himself for a final farewell.

★ ★ ★

All the cheese from Tammy's backpack was gone.

Looking at all the peck holes in the cardboard boxes, it was clear they wouldn't hold much longer. The piggy pong that had kept the pigs safe so far was lifting.

'How's your tummy feeling?' she asked hopefully.

Brian shook his head. 'There's nothing on the way.'

The army of super-chicks was bobbing up and down. Their individual peeps were swelling and combining to make one gigantic *PEEP* of fury. The chicks were getting ready for one last attack on the pigs.

'I wish my last meal ever hadn't been cheese,' said Brian.

The *PEEP* became almost unbearably loud. As it reached its highest point, the chicks swarmed forward.

★ ★ ★

Curly was panting hard when he reached the door to the incubator shed.

He looked back once across the field and saw that Mangler was flying up into the air.

But why?

Curly watched as the huge airborne chicken levelled off and then flew in a wide circle around the arena. The crowd of chickens at the arena turned their heads to follow him. As Colonel Cluck followed his prized creation, he saw that Curly was missing.

'That little runt has escaped!' he shouted.

Unfortunately there was nowhere in the field for Curly to hide. It didn't take Cluck long to spot that the missing pig was over by the incubator shed.

'Get that pig!' Cluck screamed, jabbing a stubby wing in Curly's direction.

Several chicken-troopers started running, stretching their wings ready to fly after him.

Curly fumbled with the key and slotted it into the keyhole to unlock the door. He turned the door handle and shoved. At least if he freed Tammy and Brian there'd be three of them to face their enemies.

With a final glance towards the Cockpit where Pete lay, Curly saw Mangler tuck his wings in to his sides and begin his plummet back to earth. With horror, Curly realized what the rooster was doing – a Chicken Death Dive!

But there was nothing he could do now. As the chicken-troopers rushed across the field towards him he shouldered the door open.

Curly couldn't even see Tammy and Brian or the super-chicks in the gloom of the incubator shed. He couldn't really think of anything apart from the terrible pong that hit him with the force of a runaway sewage tanker.

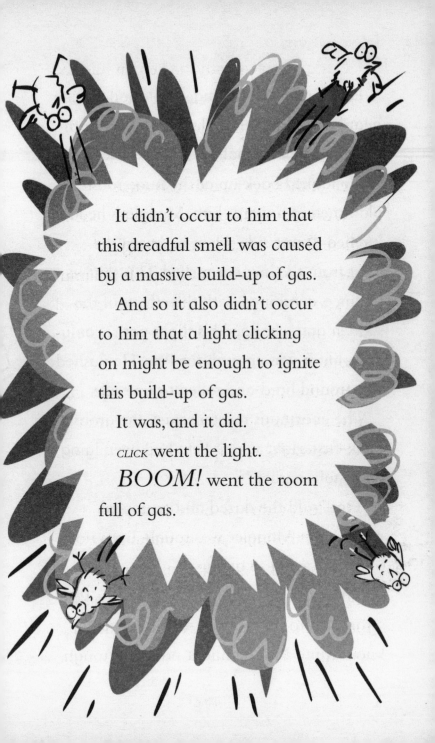

It didn't occur to him that
this dreadful smell was caused
by a massive build-up of gas.

And so it also didn't occur
to him that a light clicking
on might be enough to ignite
this build-up of gas.

It was, and it did.

CLICK went the light.

BOOM! went the room
full of gas.

Pete didn't see the huge explosion, but he heard it, and he felt a blast of hot air from the giant blue fireball.

He looked back up at the huge rooster plummeting towards him. Mangler's head lurched to one side when he heard the blast from the incubator shed. This shift in balance, combined with the effects of the sudden gust, changed his flight path – only a little, but it was enough for Pete. He pushed the ground hard and rolled to one side.

The enormous rooster struck the ground beak-first, right where Pete had been lying an instant earlier.

'Oof!' said the dazed and crumpled rooster. But Mangler was tough. Even now, he was starting to get up.

Ignoring the pains all over his body, Pete scrambled to his feet. He might not really know Kung Poo, he might not be as tough as Mangler, but he had one thing going for him – he was a big fat pig, and he did now what big fat pigs do best. He trusted his gut.

Pete charged forward and launched himself into the air.

'CANNONBALL!' he cried.

The last thing Mangler saw was a gigantic pig belly hurtling towards him. And then everything went black.

CHAPTER 9:

A Game of Chicken

The huge gas cloud burned bright, but it burned fast too. One gigantic flash and it was done. It left behind a scene of chaos and destruction as some of the surrounding buildings instantly caught fire, and alarm bells started ringing all around the base.

Tammy and Brian were slammed backwards into one corner and the force of the explosion had blown the far side of the shed off. The light and fluffy little chicks were thrown everywhere in a shower of yellow. None of them was hurt but several looked a bit singed and they were *all* a bit miffed.

The gust lifted Curly clean off his trotters and shot him backwards. Luckily, there was something to break his fall – several chicken-troopers, who were also knocked off their feet. As they staggered groggily up, they were greeted by the sight of hundreds of furious chicks swarming out of the shed, attacking anything in their path.

Over by the Cockpit, Colonel Cluck was reaching new levels of fury. 'Get them!' he screamed at the roosters around him. 'Kill those pigs! Destroy them!'

The officers around Cluck just stood and watched him.

'What are you doing? I am the Chicken Supreme!' shrieked Cluck. 'You must obey me!'

The other chickens still didn't move. It was as if they were realizing for the first time just how bonkers their leader really was.

'No,' said one at last.

Peregrine and Lola were flying over
Chicken Island in the PiPs transporter plane.

'Can you fly this thing a bit lower?'
Peregrine asked. 'It's hard to see anything.'

Lola turned around in her seat. 'Are
you complaining about my flying?' she
demanded crossly. 'Because if you are, you
can just fly this plane yourself.'

'No, no,' cried Peregrine. 'Please just watch where we're going. We're heading towards a mountain!'

Lola turned forward and steered the cargo plane above the summit of the mountain. 'I DID see it, thank you very much,' she muttered.

She and Peregrine had flown straight to the Free-Range Happy Hatchery on Chicken Island. Here they had picked up the hen in charge, Matron Peck. The stout old bird was sitting with them now, clutching her handbag and peering out of the window. She tutted whenever the plane hit an air pocket.

'So you haven't got *any* idea where they went?' asked Peregrine.

Matron Peck shook her head. 'Dearie me, no. All I know is that they set off to the south, Wing Commander.'

'But that could be almost anywhere on

Chicken Island,' said Peregrine.

'What about over there?' suggested Lola.

'Where?'

'Near that huge fireball and the plume of black smoke,' answered Lola.

'That's the army base,' Matron Peck said.

'Well, that's where we need to go,' said Peregrine, who knew his team well. 'Only a gang of right little oinkers could cause destruction like that!'

Word spread fast among the chickens that Cluck had finally gone nutty as a bag of nuts. Many of them were trying to round up the savage hordes of chicks. The rest were just standing around, scratching at the dirt and wondering what to do now.

Curly hurried over to the Cockpit, where Pete was leaning on Nugget's shoulder and limping as he tested for broken bones. Mangler was still on the ground, sleeping like a gigantic, muscular baby.

Curly grinned. 'You won!'

'I told you, kid. Sometimes you have to trust your gut.'

'But how did you know that Nugget would help us?' asked Curly.

'Easy,' said Pete. 'When he first took us to Cluck, Nugget used the phrase "quick as a chick". The only other time I'd heard that was from Matron Peck. I guessed that Nugget had come from Peck's Hatchery, so I hummed a bit of the music they play there. Just to remind him to do the right thing.'

'That's . . .' Curly was going to say 'brilliant', but instead he jerked his head round. 'Wait! Where's Cluck?'

Pete didn't care. 'What does it matter now if the fat little rooster has flown the coop?'

But then suddenly a small single-seater Chickenhawk jet appeared from one of the hangars. The pilot at the controls was

Colonel Cluck!

Cluck taxied the jet to the runway. The Chickenhawk's engines screamed, and then it zoomed off into the air.

'He's getting away!' said Curly.

Pete shrugged. 'He can't do much harm on his own.'

But the little chicken Nugget shook his

head. 'The nose-cone of that jet is packed full of concentrated Rooster Booster,' he said grimly. 'Cluck's back-up plan was to detonate it high in the sky and dose every chicken on Chicken Island.'

Curly looked to Pete. 'We have to stop him.'

Pete shook his head. 'I'm afraid *we* can't. I'd never make it to my jet in time, and Tammy and Brian aren't in any shape to fly. There's only one pig who can do something.'

It took Curly a moment to realize who Pete was talking about – him!

Tammy and Brian emerged into the light and looked at the mess the base was in.

'Incredible,' murmured Brian.

'Do you know what's *really* incredible?' Tammy said. 'The fact that your flightsuit is still perfectly clean!'

Brian looked down with pride. It was true! His flightsuit still looked freshly laundered and ironed.

Tammy noticed SkyHog 1 zipping down the runway and taking off. 'Wonder where Pete's going?' she asked.

'Um, Pete is over there, with that little chicken,' said Brian.

Tammy looked back at the plane. 'So who's flying his plane then?'

The controls of the jet felt very different from other planes he'd flown, but Curly was a born flyer. *Just stay calm*, he told himself.

He scanned the skies for a glimpse of Cluck's plane. It was only at the last minute that he realized it was flying up behind him. The Chickenhawk was fast – faster than the SkyHog – but PiPs jets were the best in the skies at fancy flying. Curly pulled it up into a sudden loop the loop, and Cluck's plane shot past below him.

Curly gulped nervously. This was his first aeroplane dogfight – well, strictly speaking it was more of a pig/chicken fight.

The Chickenhawk had gone into a wide circle, and now it was coming back this way, straight towards him. Curly was confused. What was Cluck doing? Was the little rooster absolutely bonkers? Well, yes, it did seem safe to say that the chicken was several eggs short of the full dozen.

Suddenly, Curly realized what was going on in Cluck's fowl brain – this was a game of chicken! The loser was the one who lost his nerve first and swerved away.

Curly's mind was racing. The right thing to do – the safe, sensible thing, what the *PiPs Rules and Regulations* said you had to do in a situation like this – was to swerve away.

But Curly had done enough running for one day. If this was to be his one and only

mission as a PiP, he wanted to do it in style.
He held his course.

Of course, if neither of them swerved
away, they would both be losers. There
would be nothing left of them but two
piles of stew: one chicken and one pork.

So here's the question, Curly told himself:
What would Peter Porker do?

He swept a spare pair of Pete's mirror
shades from the console and popped them
on, as if they might help provide the answer.

Unfortunately, he wasn't ready for just how dark the lenses of Pete's mirror shades were. (Pete had chosen them for maximum coolness and had then had to spend months getting his eyes used to them.)

Now Curly couldn't see anything ahead of him. Keeping one trotter on the controls, the piglet clawed at the sunglasses with the other. The glasses had hooked right round his ears and they wouldn't come off.

Curly could *see* nothing, but he could *hear* the sound of Cluck's jet ahead – coming straight at him!

Down on the ground, everybody – pigs and chickens alike – stared up at the battle of nerves in the sky.

'They're going to crash!' wailed Brian.

'Swerve, Curly, swerve!' Tammy was chanting under her breath.

Only Pete stayed calm. 'You can do it, kid,' he murmured. 'Listen to your gut.'

The moment of impact was almost upon them. Any second now the two planes would smash into each other in a gigantic fireball, and . . .

NO! At the last possible moment one of the pilots threw his plane into a dive.

'It's Cluck!' yelled Pete. 'He chickened out! I *knew* it!'

The Chickenhawk's dive was too steep to pull out of. It spiralled down, smoke pouring out of the back end. Finally, Cluck managed to get some control of it, but it was too late to level off completely. It was going to crash.

With seconds to spare, the cockpit hatch blew off and the ejector seat shot up into the air. Its parachute opened immediately. Cluck was strapped into it, and he was gripping a large canister of Rooster Booster in both wings.

As the unpiloted Chickenhawk plopped down in the marshes, Cluck floated over the base. For a while, it looked as if he might hit the roof of one of the hangars.

But then there was a huge gust of wind – completely unrelated to Brian this time – and the ejector seat landed in a large metal tank.

'What is that?' asked Tammy. 'Is it full of chicken feed?'

The little rooster Nugget was by her side. 'Not exactly. What's in that tank is what the chicken feed *ends up* as, if you get my meaning.'

'You mean it's full of . . .?'

Nugget couldn't hide his smile.

'Chicken poo.'

CHAPTER 10:

Chicken Supreme

As team medic, Brian was tending to Peter Porker's injured leg.

'Does it hurt when I press here?' he asked.

'Argh!' said Pete. When the pain had died down, he pointed at the sewage tank Cluck had landed in. 'I suppose someone ought to fish him out of there,' he said.

'The chickens can do that,' said Tammy. 'It will give them something to do, now they're not taking over the world.'

But suddenly, there was a dull thudding noise. It sounded like a pneumatic drill and it was coming from the tank.

The hammering grew louder and louder, and then suddenly a feathered fist punched a hole straight through the metal walls of the tank. A jet of chicken poo gushed out.

'Nooooooo!' wailed Brian as a big dollop landed all over his flightsuit. Something ripped the hole wider and leapt out. Colonel Cluck was not looking good. For one thing, he was covered from head to toe in muck. But that wasn't all – the canister of concentrated Rooster Booster had come open and mixed with the contents of the tank. Cluck had absorbed it all – more Rooster Booster than any chicken alive.

He was still
no taller, but
now he was
a solid ball of
pure muscle.
He looked
unbelievably
strong. And
there was only
one thing on his
mind now – revenge

against the pigs who had ruined his plans.

His single yellow eye bulged as it spotted
the PiPs. He sprang towards them, swatting
aside a pair of chicken-troopers who got in
his way.

It was clear who was the main target of
his hatred – Peter Porker.

'You've ruined everything!' Cluck spat.
'But I'll have my revenge! I'll turn you into
sausages! I'll –'

The rooster was so angry he didn't even notice the sound of a different plane overhead.

He bounded closer to Pete. 'I'll roast you on a spit! I'll –'

'Erm, I think you'd better look up!' said Tammy.

'Do you think I am an IDIOT?' roared Cluck. 'I'm not a stupid pig! I AM THE CHICKEN SUPREME –'

It was only when a shadow crossed over him that it finally occurred to Colonel Cluck that Tammy might not be lying. He looked up to see the biscuit-fed bulk of Peregrine Oinks-Gruntington parachuting down towards him. The Wing Commander's giant moustache fluttered proudly in the breeze.

Moments before impact, Peregrine tucked his legs up.

'CANNONBALL!' he yelled.

And then he landed right on top of Colonel Cluck.

SPLAT! The little rooster's plans for world domination were over.

'I don't think that move's in the PiPs rulebook, is it, Wing Commander?' asked Tammy.

Peregrine unstrapped his chute and looked down at the little rooster. Cluck was holding his head and groaning.

'Sometimes you have to bend the rules,' Peregrine said. 'Isn't that right, Captain Porker?'

Up in the skies, Curly went into a victory roll in SkyHog 1, while Lola began her descent towards the runway.

The only pig not feeling too happy was Brian, who dabbed at his flightsuit with a tissue.

'Hope you don't want a ride back in my plane, Bri,' said Tammy sympathetically.

CHAPTER 11:

A New PiP

A few days later on Pig Island, the PiPs were standing to attention in their dress uniforms.

'After his magnificent performance on Chicken Island, it gives me pleasure to induct a new member to our team. Step forward, Mr McHoglet,' said Peregrine.

Curly looked fit to burst with pride.

'Welcome to the PiPs,' said Peregrine, and he pinned the silver PiPs badge on to Curly's smart new PiPs jacket.

The young pig had dreamed of this moment. He looked down at the badge's image of wings and the Latin words: *Porci volare possunt.*

Pigs CAN fly.

'Is there anything you'd like to say?' beamed Peregrine.

Curly's eyes watered. 'Yes,' he said. 'The pin is sticking into my chest.'

* * *

After the ceremony, there was a small party.

Peregrine was explaining to the others what had been happening on Chicken Island. 'As soon as Matron Peck arrived, the chicks all calmed down and did what she told them. She's a tough old bird. She took all of the chicks back to the Free-Range Happy Hatchery. Apparently, she's had a lot of help from Nugget, and also from your old opponent, Pete.'

'You mean Mangler?' asked the captain, who was still limping a bit after that fight.

Peregrine nodded. 'Only now he prefers to go by his real name – Walter.'

Brian pushed his glasses up his snout. 'I've managed to reverse the effects of the Rooster Booster with an antidote,' he said. 'It was quite simple – just a matter of creating a 3-D model of the Booster's molecular structure and then . . .'

Brian went on to describe the ins and

outs of how he had devised an antidote.
Eight minutes later he said, 'And that's how
it worked. Isn't that fascinating?'

'Amazing,' said Tammy, who had been
reading the newspaper.

'Good work!' said Peregrine, who had
been looking out of the window.

'What? Where am I?' said Pete, jolting
awake when Lola elbowed him in the ribs.

'There's one thing I'd like to know,' said
Curly. 'What happened to Colonel Cluck?'

Tammy held up her newspaper. The front
page showed a picture of Cluck behind bars.
The headline read:

WHY DID THE CHICKEN CROSS
THE ROAD?

TO GO TO JAIL

Tammy smiled as she returned to
munching her way through the food
troughs on the table. When she reached
the chocolate biscuits, she looked up at

Peregrine. 'Hey, if you aren't going on missions any more, you'll be free to eat as many biscuits as you want, won't you?'

Peregrine nodded. 'Ye—'

Lola cleared her throat noisily.

'Actually,' said Peregrine hurriedly, 'I think I'll stick with this celery that Lola has specially prepared by . . . er, putting it raw on to a plate.'

Curly helped himself to some dessert, then offered the dish to Brian. 'Would you like some of this?' he asked. 'It's Strawberry Surprise.'

Brian let out a cry of horror at these words and hopped backwards. He bumped straight into Peregrine and there was the sound of something crunching in the Wing Commander's pocket. A pile of biscuit crumbs fell to the floor.

Pete grinned. 'I'd have thought you couldn't face another chocolate biscuit,' he said to Peregrine.

'Why?' asked the Wing Commander.

Pete's grin widened. 'Didn't you see *You've Made a Right Pig's Ear of That!* on TV last night?'

'What?' asked Peregrine. He turned to Lola. 'What's he talking about?'

Lola shrugged. 'How do you think we paid for all this food?' she said.

Peregrine was purple again – as purple as the new trousers Lola was wearing. However, when he finally thought of

something to say, nobody heard him
because:

*KWEEEEEEEEEEEEEEEEEEEEEE-
EEEEEEEEEEEEEEEEEEEP!*

It was the Alarm Squeal. Somewhere
in Animal Paradise, there was another
emergency. Someone needed help; it was
another job for the Pigs in Planes.

'Party's over,' shouted Peregrine. 'PiPs are
GO!'

The assembled pigs had already dropped
their plates. They were running towards

the SkyHog jets on the runway, and the newest member of the team, young Curly McHoglet, was in the lead, his PiPs badge glinting in the sun.

READ MORE OiNKCREDiBLY FUNNY ADVENTURES OF THE

PUFFIN

Crossword

Across→

2. A baby pig.

4. He's a little chicken with a big heart.

5. A fighting arena and where a pilot sits.

8. The secret to how pigs fly! (Clue: a kind of jet.)

9. Fluffy chicks are this colour.

11. This food gives Brian wind.

12. They've been going missing on Chicken Island.

Down ↓

1. Peregrine's favourite snack.

3. The Matron on Chicken Island.

6. Kung ___ is Pete's favourite martial art.

7. _____ Booster.

10. The PiPs radio operator.

*Turn to page 150 for the answers.

Wordsearch

Find the words opposite hidden in this grid.
(Look carefully – some may be
backwards or diagonal!)

M	R	B	A	I	H	A	S	G	O	L	F	E	C	C
P	I	E	A	A	H	O	T	Q	R	V	X	A	G	S
F	S	A	D	R	W	E	N	I	E	X	R	W	R	I
E	E	K	T	A	E	A	L	D	T	S	I	D	L	E
E	S	A	D	W	S	L	T	O	N	Z	E	F	U	N
S	L	I	T	D	E	B	S	T	F	A	L	A	X	A
E	H	A	S	H	W	L	N	T	I	Z	Q	N	E	M
M	I	E	S	I	E	A	D	O	B	C	V	E	S	S
R	O	G	N	N	W	R	K	O	E	G	L	X	I	T
R	G	G	O	E	X	E	N	O	M	Q	B	T	F	E
E	S	L	U	P	O	R	K	E	R	U	E	T	J	K
D	O	K	T	G	O	Z	S	N	G	I	V	D	T	E
C	O	E	R	I	O	J	E	E	E	Z	C	R	O	I
V	X	N	A	P	F	G	I	H	L	S	P	E	S	B
H	F	T	R	T	A	I	M	S	K	M	P	E	E	E

*Turn to page 150 for the answers.

146

BEAK   PIGPEN

COLONEL   PORKER

EGGSHELL   SNOUT

FEATHER   TWEET

HEN   WINGS

147

Word Scramble

Unscramble these words:

1. **GREERENIP**

2. **TUGGEN**

3. **KLCCU**

4. **ETRRTOT**

5. SJTE

6. YRLUC

7. ELRGMAN

8. HRAEHTYC

9. PLEAN

10. OTSRROE

* Turn to page 150 for the answers.

Answers

Crossword

Crossword grid:
- 2 Across: PIGLET
- 1 Down: BISCUIT
- 3 Down: PECS
- 4 Across: NUGGET
- 5 Across: COCKPIT
- 6 Down: STOOL (PIT... POOL)
- 7 Down: ROOSTER
- 8 Across: SKYHOG
- 9 Across: YELLOW
- 10 Down: LOLA
- 11 Across: CHEESE
- 12 Across: EGGS

Wordsearch

```
M R B A I H A S G O L F E C C
P I E A A H O T Q R V X A G S
F S A D R W E N I E X R W R I
E E K T A E A L D T S I D L E
E S A D W S L T O N Z E F U N
S L I T D E B S T F A L A X A
E H A S H W L N T I Z Q N E M
M I E S I E A D O B C V E S S
R O G N N W R K O E G L X I T
R G G O E X E N O M Q B T F E
E S L U P O R K E R U E T J K
D O K T G O Z S N G I V D T E
C O E R I O J E E E Z C R O I
V X N A P F G I H L S P E S B
H F T R T A I M S K M P E E E
```

Word Scramble

1. PEREGRINE
2. NUGGET
3. CLUCK
4. TROTTER
5. JETS
6. CURLY
7. MANGLER
8. HATCHERY
9. PLANE
10. ROOSTER